Patrick and Emma Lou

By Nan Holcomb

Illustrated by Dot Yoder

Jason & Nordic Publishers
Hollidaysburg, Pennsylvania

Revised art edition. Third printing.

Library of Congress Cataloging in Publication Data

Holcomb, Nan, date —
        Patrick and Emma Lou
Summary: Despite his excitement over walking with a new walker, three-year-old Patrick finds it isn't easy and becomes discouraged until his new friend, six-year-old Emma Lou who has spina bifida, helps him discover something important about himself.
        1. Physically handicapped — Fiction. 2. Cerebral palsy — Fiction. 3. Spina bifida — Fiction. 4. Self-acceptance — Fiction.
I. Yoder, Dot, date — ill.
II Title.
PZ7.H6972Pat 1989   [E]   88-35769

Paper: ISBN 0-944727-03-4
Hardbound: ISBN 0-944727-14-X

Printed in the United States of America on acid free paper

for Michael
  who shared his first walk with us

This Monday morning Patrick was ready
for physical therapy. But, this Monday
morning he had to wait because...

Miss Jones and Fred were very late.
Patrick stared at Emma Lou. He stared at
her legs and he stared at her braces.
Emma Lou stuck out her tongue.

At last the door opened and Fred said,
"We're ready when you are."
Mommy said, "Good-bye. Now really try."
Fred pushed Patrick through the doorway.
Patrick didn't feel quite as ready as before.

Emma Lou finally got herself off the
chair, pulled herself up in her walker and
WALKED through the door.

Emma Lou went straight to the parallel bars.
Fred picked Patrick up and set him on
the floor.

Emma Lou did pull ups on the bar.
"Let's see you pull yourself up. You do
that and we're ready to go!" Miss Jones
said, holding a brand new walker. "Hand
over hand and up you go!"
Patrick pulled and he pulled and...

he did it! He stood up.

"Look, Fred! Look, Emma Lou! Patrick did it!"

Patrick grinned and his knees jiggled then...

"Hurray!" they all cheered him.

"Whoa, wait a minute! You can't walk with
your hands tight together and your feet in
a bunch. Let's move this foot a bit — just so.
There, that's better. Put one hand on this
handle and one over there." Miss Jones
held the walker until Patrick was ready.

"Now, nice and easy and don't forget to steer! Lift a foot and put it down — just like we've practiced."

"Lift a foot and put it down." Patrick moved out — just like Emma Lou.

"Steer! Steer!" Miss Jones yelled.

CRASH!

BUMP!

The walker hit the wall and...

14

Patrick's bottom **hit the floor!**

"Well, let's not sit here," Miss Jones said.
"Let's get up and try some more!"

Patrick gave her a mean look and pulled
himself back up. Legs apart — one hand
here and one hand there — now...

Lift a foot and put it down.

"Steer! Steer!" Fred yelled and Miss
Jones held out her hands, but...

Patrick looked up too late. The walker
bumped into the slant board and...

Patrick's bottom **hit the floor.**

"You've got to look up. Not at the floor,"
Fred said. "Now, up you go and try some
more."

That's easy to say, but it's my bottom
that's getting sore, Patrick thought.

Hand over hand — stand — and go. Lift a
foot and put it down.

"Steer! Steer!"

He ran into Emma Lou doing push-ups
on the floor.

Jiggle-jiggle. Patrick's legs felt like
rubber. He held on tighter.

"Don't fall!" yelled Emma Lou. "Hang on tight!"

"Good job! You did all right," Fred said.
   "I'm so proud of you!" Miss Jones picked
him up and put him in his chair. "Go home
and practice hard. We'll see you next week."

The next week Patrick rested on the mat and watched Emma Lou walk between the bars.

"Yeaa-a-ay," they all cheered.

Emma Lou reached the end...

and down she went.
    Emma Lou's bottom hit the floor!
    Patrick scowled. Walking wasn't easy.
Why can't we just walk like other kids
without all this trouble.

24

Just me and Emma Lou walking easy like
other kids do. I'd hold her hand and she'd
hold mine.

"Time to go to work, Patrick. Rest time is
over. Up you go," Miss Jones held his walker.

"You and Emma Lou are going for a walk down the hall."

Hand over hand — stand up straight. Lift a foot and put it down.

Patrick led the way out the door. Eyes up — not at the floor.

"Well, look who's walking," Miss Sims,
the speech teacher said.

Patrick stood taller and smiled his best
smile...and then he forgot.

"Hey, watch out!"

BANG!!
CRASH!!!
Patrick and Emma Lou were all in a heap.

28

Patrick looked at Emma Lou.

Emma Lou didn't look pleased!

Patrick closed his eyes.

Why can't we be like other kids? We'd run and jump and maybe even climb trees?

Patrick put his forehead on the floor and waited to see if he could sprout wings and fly or somebody would pick him up and carry him away or...

WOW!!!
WHAT WAS THAT?
A KISS!!

He turned his head, and looked into Emma Lou's eyes.

Emma Lou smiled. "Why can't we be like other kids? Because you're just you, Patrick and I'm just me!"

Patrick thought about that.

Then Patrick smiled back.

I like you, Emma Lou... and...I like me!

And that's good, Emma Lou. That's good!